For Sam, Linnea, and Wallace.
May you follow your own voices, too. — D.R.

Big thanks to my assistant/husband Wenchen. — R.Q.

Greystone Kids / Greystone Books Ltd.
greystonebooks.com

Cataloguing data available from Library and Archives Canada
ISBN 978-1-77164-785-4 (cloth)
ISBN 978-1-77164-786-1 (epub)

FSC
www.fsc.org

MIX
Paper from
responsible sources
FSC® C016973

Editing by Kallie George
Copy editing by Becky Noelle
Proofreading by Doeun Rivendell
Jacket and text design by Sara Gillingham Studio

The illustrations in this book were made in Procreate on an iPad.

Printed and bound in Singapore on FSC® certified paper at COS Printers Pte Ltd.
The FSC® label means that materials used for the product have been responsibly sourced.

We thank Dr. Mirjam Knörnschild for her research on the development of echolocation in
bat pups, and for her comments on an earlier draft of this book.

Greystone Books gratefully acknowledges the Musqueam, Squamish, and Tsleil-Waututh
peoples on whose land our Vancouver head office is located.

Greystone Books thanks the Canada Council for the Arts, the British Columbia Arts Council,
the Province of British Columbia through the Book Publishing Tax Credit, and the
Government of Canada for supporting our publishing activities.

FIONA THE FRUIT BAT

BY *Dan Riskin*   ILLUSTRATED BY *Rachel Qiuqi*

GREYSTONE KIDS

GREYSTONE BOOKS • VANCOUVER/BERKELEY/LONDON

It was finally time for Fiona's first flight,
but Fiona didn't feel ready.

It was too dark!
What if she hit a wall or got lost?
How was she supposed to fly
when she couldn't see a thing?

She took a deep breath
and opened her wings . . .

Mama called out from a shadow nearby:
"Fiona, remember . . . LISTEN."

Then Mama unhooked her feet and was gone.

Listen to what? It made no sense.

But Fiona didn't know what else to do,

so she hung from the ceiling
and twisted her body,
pointing her big round ears
in every direction.

takka-takka-tik

Fiona heard many of the sounds she was used to.

The steady **bibble-babble-bubble** far away,

a **SPLAT, SPLAT, SPLAT** down below,

and a very faint **takka-takka-tik** nearby.

Although Fiona couldn't see what made those sounds,
they were familiar. They made her feel safe.

But how would listening help her fly?
What was Mama talking about?

bibble-babble-bubble

SPLAT, SPLAT, SPLAT

Fiona missed being carried by Mama.
She missed the stars in the sky,
the smell of the fruits that Mama ate,
and the taste of warm milk.

What if she never learned to fly?
Would she ever go outside again?

Fiona sniffled, then started to whimper.

That's when Fiona heard a new sound—

a faint whisper.

She stopped, aimed her ears, and listened,

but the sound was already gone.

The calls of a bat interrupted the silence.

It was her best friend Cassie.
Cassie was chewing, and Fiona could smell the ripe fruit.
She imagined what it would taste like.

"I wish you'd come have some!" said Cassie,
and she flew out of the cave for more.

Fiona called out after her
but was too scared to follow.

The new sound came back again.
But this time, it was louder.
Fiona whipped her ears upward to meet it.

And then something very strange happened . . .

Somehow, that sliver of sound
made a shape appear in her mind.

But before she could make out what it was,
the sound was gone.

The cave was quiet again,
until another bat swooped in.

It was Mama!
She landed gracefully against Fiona's side,
folded up her wings,
and licked her daughter's face.

Fiona was grumpy about being left alone,
but that didn't last.

A cuddle was exactly what she needed.

As Mama cleaned Fiona's fur,
Fiona smelled a new fruit on her breath—
one she'd never smelled before.

She pulled herself onto Mama's chest to be carried,
but Mama gently pushed her back.

"My love, you're too big!
I know you can fly on your own.
Remember . . . LISTEN."
Mama licked Fiona's head,
then dropped away and flew out of the cave.

Fiona was alone once more.
She started to wail.

Suddenly, Fiona heard the sound again.
She realized it was the call of a bat.

It wasn't Cassie or Mama,
but the voice was familiar . . . who was it?

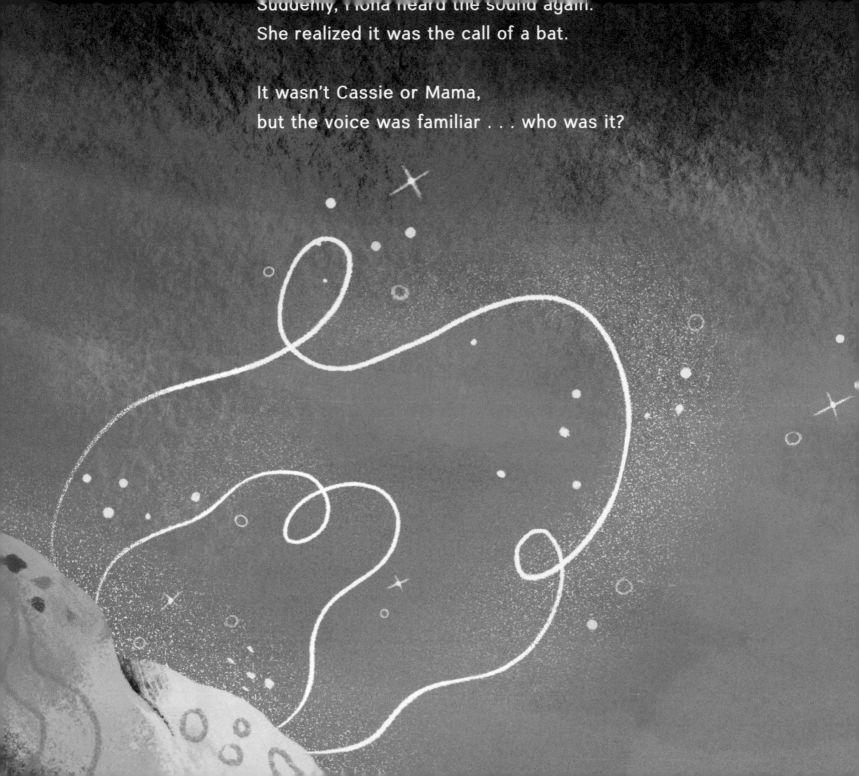

It didn't come close, but it kept calling.
She listened as hard as she could.
Then, like before, she saw an image in her head.

Fiona turned her head to hear.
More images came as she whimpered.
Edges and corners came and went like lightning.
Did these shapes connect somehow?

And as she focused, she noticed . . .
the sound was crying!

Was some other bat lonely?
Was some other bat hurt?
Fiona had to do something!

So she stopped her own sniffling, took a deep breath,
then said in a loud and clear voice:

"IT'S OKAY. I WILL HELP YOU. YOU WILL BE ALRIGHT."

"IT'S OKAY," replied the voice.

"I WILL HELP YOU."

"YOU WILL BE ALRIGHT."

It wasn't another bat!
It was her own echo!

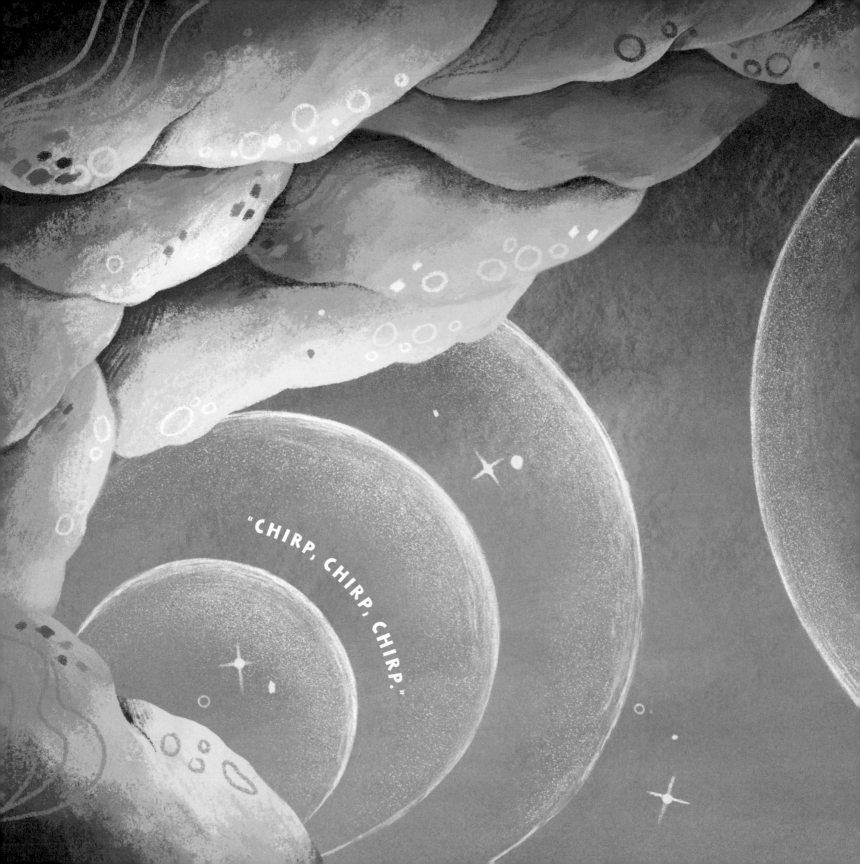

Fiona called out loudly: "**CHIRP, CHIRP, CHIRP.**"

And three echoes came back, showing Fiona the far wall of the cave.

Now she knew what those shapes were.

Each one was an outline of the things her voice had touched.

takka-takka-tik

Fiona called out again, and everything snapped into focus.

She saw water running down to the floor.
She watched a creature hopping through a puddle
and a skinny little animal walking on the wall.

For the first time,
Fiona could see her home.
She wouldn't hit a wall.
She wouldn't get lost.

She felt different now, excited—
from the ends of her ears
up to the tips of her toes.

SPLAT, SPLAT, SPLAT

bibble-babble-bubble

Fiona didn't need her mother to carry her
or Cassie to lead her.
Fiona was ready to follow her own voice.

She took a deep breath,
unhooked her feet, listened . . .

CHIRP

CHIRP

CHIRP

. . . and was gone.

What Is Echolocation?

Echolocation is the main way that bats like Fiona perceive the world around them. A bat calls out several times per second in short little bursts and listens carefully. Some of the sound bounces off nearby objects and comes back toward the bat. That returning sound is called an echo, and when the bat hears an echo, it knows the sound must have hit something. In other words, the bat uses **echoes** to **locate** the things around itself: it **echolocates**!

Are bats blind? Not at all! If there's enough light, bats like Fiona can see with their eyes just fine, but since they live in dark caves during the day, and come out at night, there's usually not very much light available. Echolocation works equally well no matter how dark it is, so it's much more convenient.

A bat using echolocation probably builds a picture of the world in its mind based on **echoes**, just like most humans do when they see things with their eyes. But there's one important difference: with echolocation, you can't see colors! A red object and a blue object make identical **echoes**, so with echolocation, they seem exactly the same.

Even though there's no color, echolocation can reveal vivid details about texture. The texture of a surface changes how the sound bounces off of it. Hard and flat surfaces, like the wall of Fiona's cave (or the cover of this book), reflect sound loudly and mostly unchanged, while a soft surface, like the edge of a bushy tree (or a pillow), reflects an echo that's quite different from the original sound. Bats quickly figure out the differences among those **echoes** to tell different objects apart.

Learning to Echolocate

Baby bats like Fiona (called "pups") make lots of noises to communicate with their mothers, or with other bats, but they don't figure out echolocation until about the same time they learn to fly, at around three weeks of age. Although a bat has been hearing other bats echolocate its whole life, it can't use the **echoes** of other bats to perceive the world. It has to learn to pay attention to the **echoes** of its own voice, just like Fiona did.

Try It Yourself!

You can echolocate, just like Fiona!

Cover your eyes with a bandana (or just close them tight) and give it a try. You can click your tongue, sing, or just say your name. Have someone move this book back and forth in front of your face, and see if you can tell when it's in front of you. Next, have them switch between this book and a pillow, and see if you can tell the difference. Some people who can't see use echolocation to navigate every day. They may even echolocate to avoid obstacles while riding a bike! All it takes is practice!

About Fiona

Bats are incredibly diverse. There are more than 1,400 different species in the world. Fiona belongs to a species called *Carollia perspicillata*, the "short-tailed fruit bat." They're very common in the tropical rainforests of Central and South America.

Fiona's species is in a family of bats called the leaf-nosed bats. They have that name because most of them (Fiona included) have a cute little flap of skin around the nostrils that looks kind of like a leaf.

Short-tailed fruit bats eat many different kinds of fruit, but they have a problem: on any given night in the rainforest, it's hard to know which kind of fruit is available, and it would take a long time to visit every possible fruit tree each night. Their solution? Smell the breath of other bats coming home to the cave. That way they can learn which fruit is available and head straight for the trees with fruit, skipping the ones that have none. You've probably noticed that Fiona's very good at smelling what other bats have been eating. That will serve her well as she learns to find food on her own.